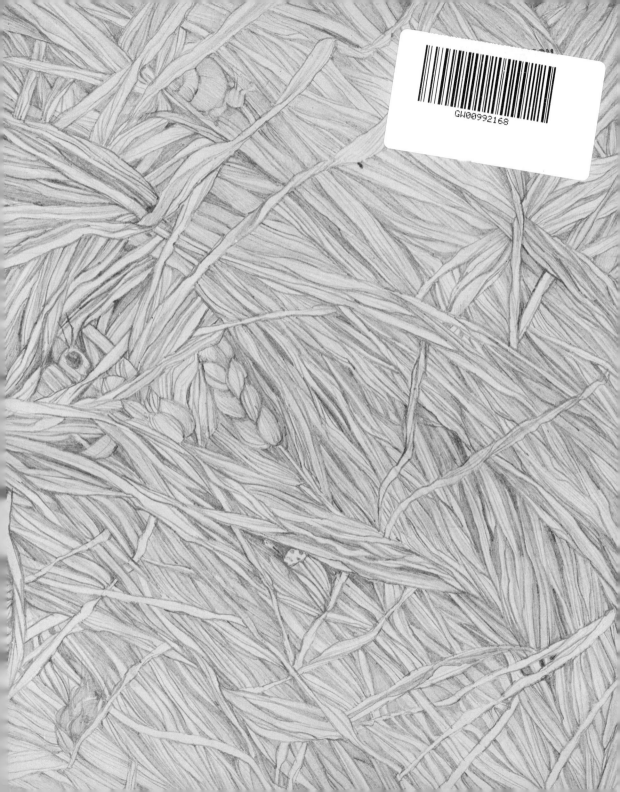

A Colonial Williamsburg Tale

The Mouse and the Mill

By Alma S. Coon

Illustrated by Kathryn E. Shoemaker

Published by The Colonial Williamsburg Foundation
Williamsburg, Virginia

There's a bundle of straw
Stacked up 'round a pole
Down in the dell on a big bumpy knoll.
A bundle of straw
Is a good place
to hide —
Just for me. I live inside.

Some corn and a seed.
That's all I need.

And a berry and such.
Not very much.

From my home in the straw,
    I can look up and see
My friend, the old windmill,
    Shadowing me.

The sails of the mill
    Reach for the sky,
Waiting for wind to turn —
    To fly!

The wind is a friend,
    A friend indeed,
Helping the mill
    Grind flour from seed.

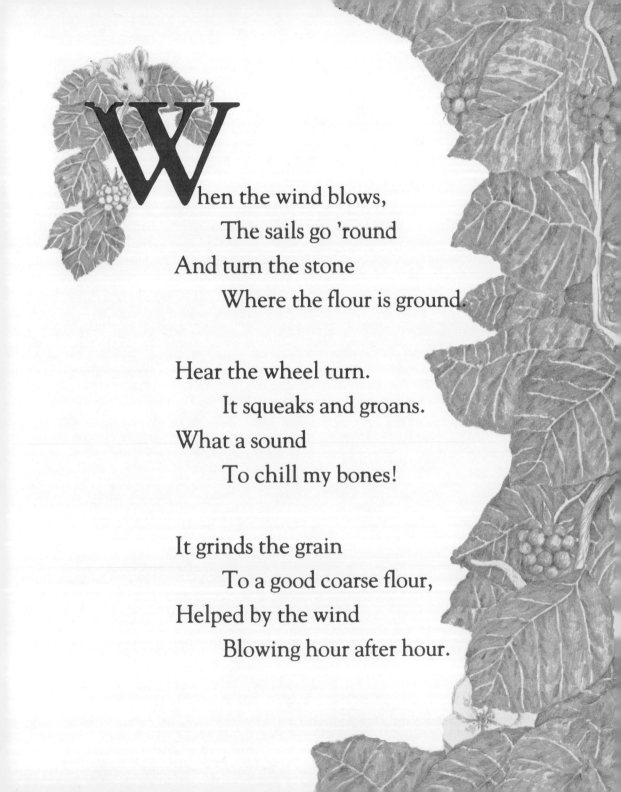

When the wind blows,
    The sails go 'round
And turn the stone
    Where the flour is ground.

Hear the wheel turn.
    It squeaks and groans.
What a sound
    To chill my bones!

It grinds the grain
    To a good coarse flour,
Helped by the wind
    Blowing hour after hour.

At dusk I wait
    Till the windmill is still,
And bustle myself
    Up the scraggly
    hill.

I'm quiet as only a mouse
    Can be
In the shadowy twilight
    When no one can see.

There goes the miller
    Home to his bed.
With the flour he carries,
    His wife bakes their bread.

The old miller's oxen
  Chew their hay.
Their burdens were heavy.
  They've had a long day.

The air is warm.
Their rough hide twitches.
They fling their tails
Up like switches.

They treat me as if
  I were cousin or kin,
And pay no mind
  As I scurry in.

My mill! My own larder
       All to myself.
The whole windmill floor
       Is a big pantry shelf!

With kernels of corn
       Dropped down from the stone,
More than enough
       For one mouse alone.

Some corn and a seed.
That's all I need.

And a berry and such.
Not very much.

I fill my cheeks with the tiny
         Grains,
Then hurry right home before it
         Rains.

The hollyhocks guard the fence
         All night.
I slip past the gate that's locked
         So tight.

I stop.
I sniff.
As the scent of a rose
Itches and twitches my dark, shiny nose.

The crickets are thrumming
    Their same old song.
I'd better get home
    Where I belong.

To the bundle of straw
Stacked up 'round a pole
Down in the dell on a big bumpy knoll.

That warm and cosy place
to hide,
Just right for me. I live inside.

Now look inside.
What do you see?
Four baby Sparrows chirping with glee.

Safe in their bottle until they have grown.
'Til it's time to be shown how to fly on their own.

To fly from the bottle that hangs on the wall.
There should be snug bottles
In gardens for all!

The mother bird flies back, frightened and fierce
Straight at the man, her beak to pierce.

He speaks to her softly.
He wants to tell
That the four tiny babies
Are safe and well.

The sounds from the bottle sound good to her ear.
She flies to the rim.
All are safe! It's clear.

The man spies the bottle down on the ground,
And checks to see that the babies are sound.

Carefully, gently, the man so tall
Places the bottle right back on the wall.

Now, what's all the clamor?
A man with a hammer?

He's striking a nail right in the wall!
Now the bottle is certain to fall!

There it goes, down to the ground.
What a terrible, terrible sound!
Our babies are going to lose their nest.
A bottle can't stand that kind of test.

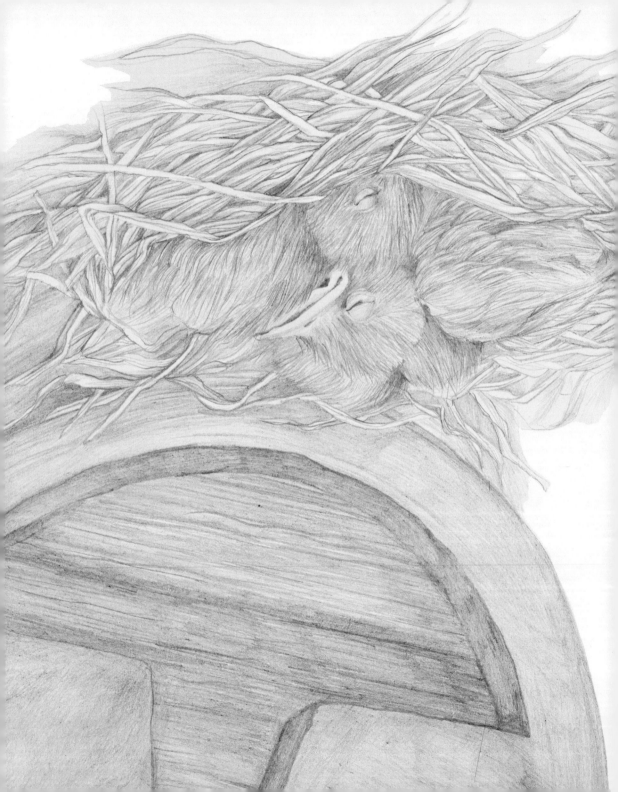

How snug and dry.
I can see why.
It's a tight place to be.
Look again and you'll see.

SPARROWS!
Four baby birds tucked in tight.
See the heads?
Hear the squeaks
When they open their beaks?

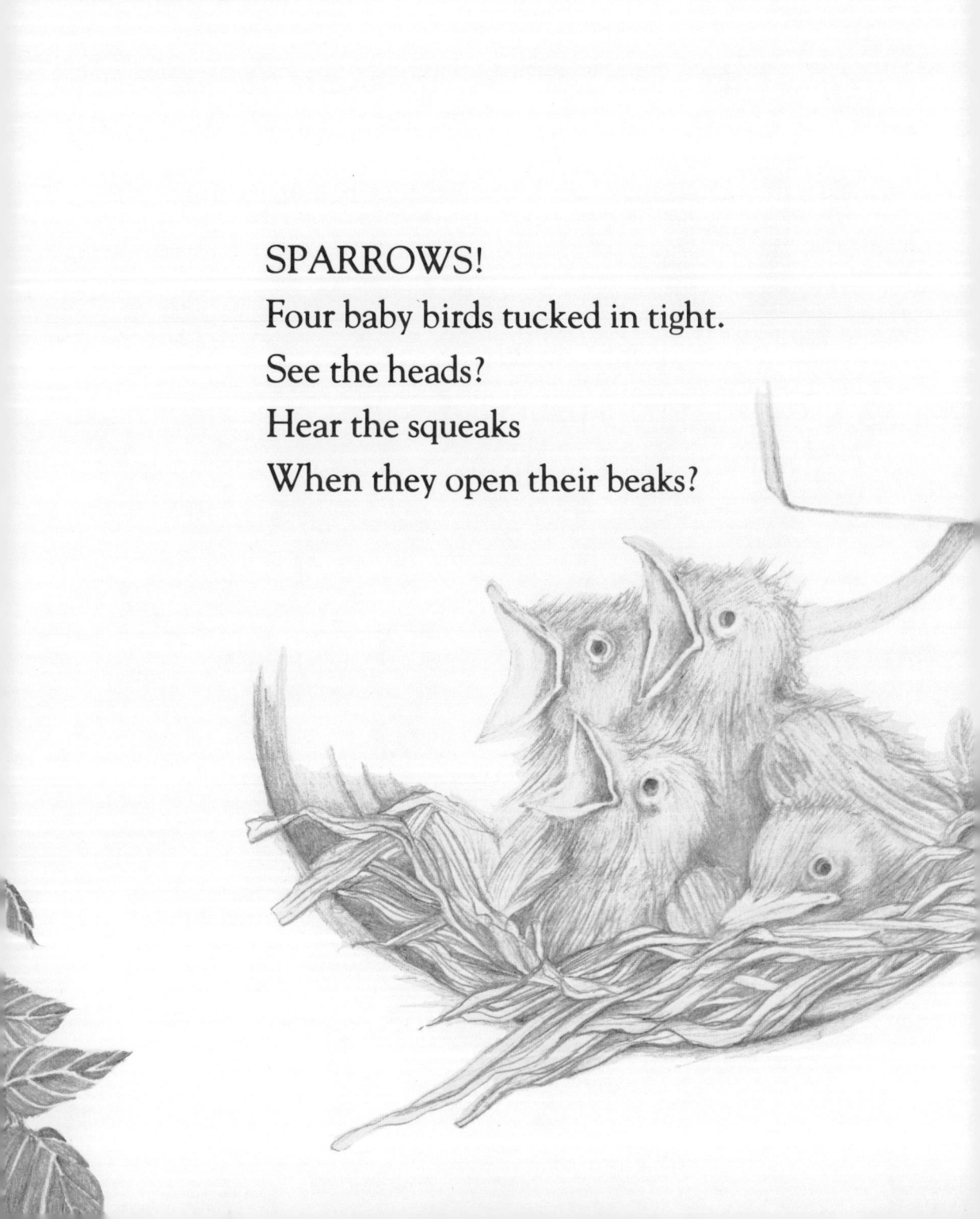

ou say a Jay?
A Jay's too big to hide inside.

A Crow?
Heaven's no!

A Thrush?
They like brush.
Then what?

Look inside.
What do you see?
It's too dark to tell.
Well?

What do you see?
One? Two? Three? Four?
Any more?

What do you see?
Baby Birds!
That's something I've never heard.

There's a shiny brown bottle on the wall
        Up high.
See how it catches light from the sky?

The bottle's a house where birds can live.
A special house with warmth to give.

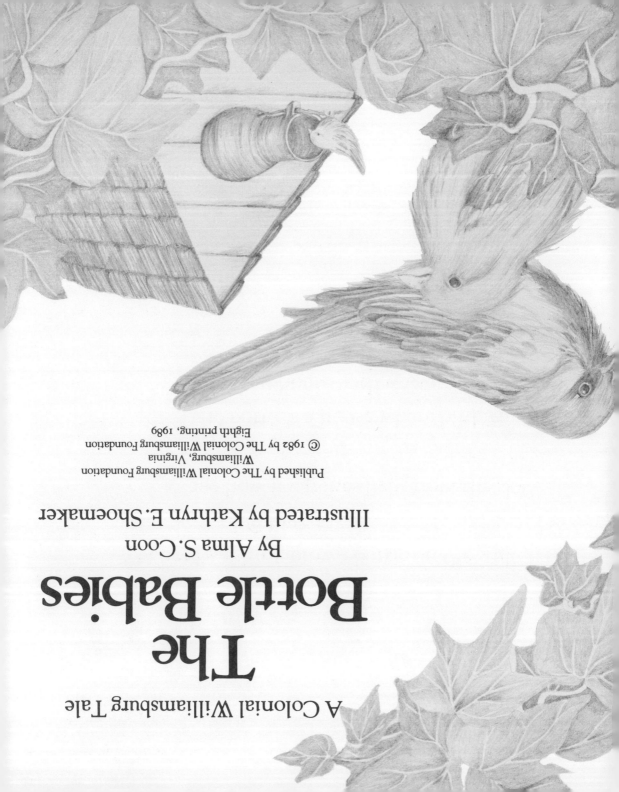

A Colonial Williamsburg Tale

The Bottle Babies

By Alma S. Coon
Illustrated by Kathryn E. Shoemaker

Published by The Colonial Williamsburg Foundation
Williamsburg, Virginia
© 1982 by The Colonial Williamsburg Foundation
Eighth printing, 1989